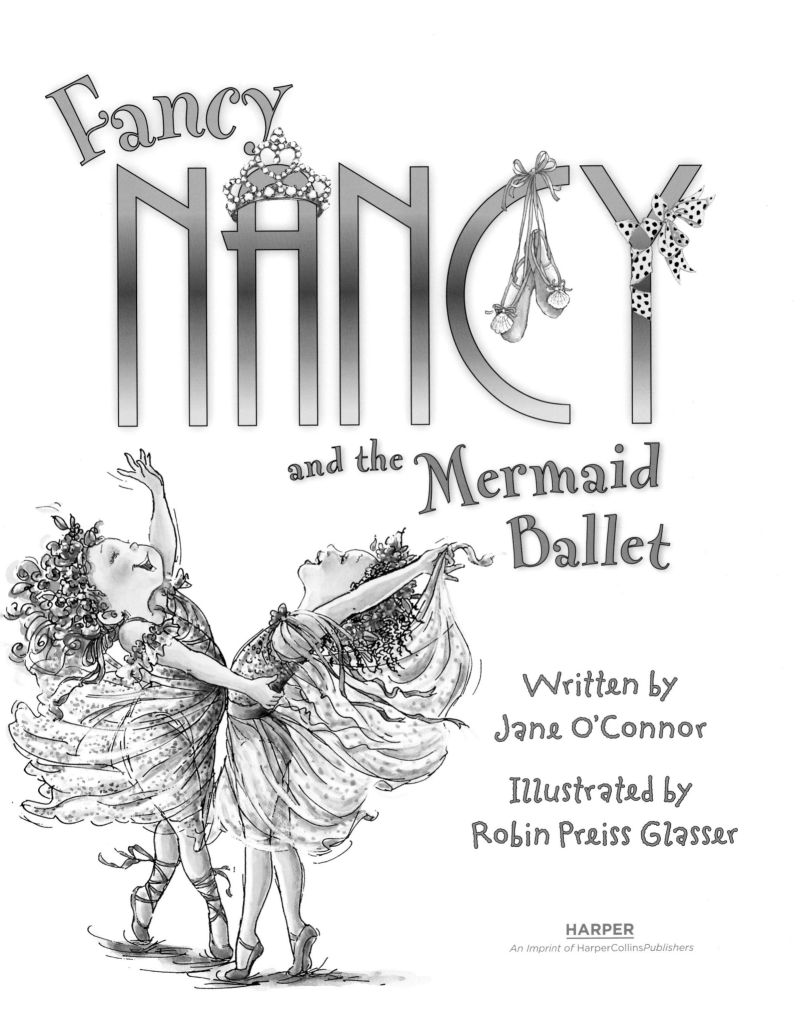

Fancy NANCY and the Mermaid Ballet

Written by
Jane O'Connor

Illustrated by
Robin Preiss Glasser

HARPER
An Imprint of HarperCollinsPublishers

To J.O'C. from J.O'C., with all my heart!

For Jane—with gratitude for creating this world, which has changed mine
—R.P.G.

Merci to Savanah, the winner of the Fancy Nancy Fantastic Fan Photo Contest,
and her family for allowing us to include her super-spiffy likeness in the Mermaid Ballet.

Fancy Nancy and the Mermaid Ballet
Text copyright © 2012 by Jane O'Connor
Illustrations copyright © 2012 by Robin Preiss Glasser
All rights reserved. Printed in the United States of America.
No part of this book may be used or reproduced in any manner whatsoever without
written permission except in the case of brief quotations embodied in critical articles and reviews.
For information address HarperCollins Children's Books, a division of HarperCollins Publishers,
10 East 53rd Street, New York, NY 10022.
www.harpercollinschildrens.com

Library of Congress Cataloging-in-Publication Data

O'Connor, Jane.
Fancy Nancy and the mermaid ballet / written by Jane O'Connor ; illustrated by Robin Preiss Glasser. — 1st ed.
p. cm.
ISBN 978-0-06-170381-2 (trade bdg.) — ISBN 978-0-06-170382-9 (lib. bdg.)
[1. Ballet—Fiction. 2. Friendship—Fiction. 3. Vocabulary—Fiction.] I. Glasser, Robin Preiss, ill. II. Title.
PZ7.O222Facs 2012   2011019373
[E]—dc23   CIP
                                                                                              AC

Typography by Jeanne L. Hogle
11 12 13 14 15 16 CG/WOR 10 9 8 7 6 5 4 3 2 1

First Edition

I have thrilling news—thrilling means terrific and exciting all mixed together.

"We're going to be in a ballet!" I tell my mom and JoJo. "It's called *Deep-Sea Dances.*"

I am positive—that's fancy for 100 percent sure—that
Madame Lucille will pick Bree and me to be mermaids.

We play mermaids all the time. JoJo's kiddie pool
is our lagoon—a lagoon is a fancy kind of lake.

We pretend that our clubhouse is called Mermaid Mansion. (Mansions are almost as big and fancy as castles.) Our mermaid names are Turquoise and Sapphire, which are fancy shades of blue.

Here is my mermaid costume. I designed it myself.

The night before dance class, I perform for everyone.
Not to brag, but I am the most graceful person in my family.

Ta-da! I make my grand entrance.

I do leaps that are called *jetés* . . .

and knee bends that are called *pliés*.

Don't you love how so many ballet words are in French?

"Ooh, maybe Madame Lucille will make me head mermaid." Then I lower my voice. "Of course, I'll feel terrible if I end up with a bigger part than Bree."

"Nancy, remember—being in a ballet is thrilling no matter what part you have."

I nod. I guess my mom is worrying that Bree won't get a good part too.

Today I hardly wobble at all when I balance on one leg.

And I am almost positive that Rhonda bumped into me, not the other way around.

Twice Madame Lucille says I am making progress—that is fancy for getting better.

I say, "Merci, Madame."
Then I curtsy in the special ballet way.

At the end of class, Madame Lucille
announces the parts. Bree and I sit together.
All my fingers are crossed.

I can hardly stand the suspense!

At pickup time, I tell my dad the awful news. "I am a tree."
"And I'm just an oyster," Bree says.
My dad acts like this is so thrilling.

"Dad, you don't understand. My costume will
be BROWN," I explain. "There is no way to look
fancy in brown."

Later we have a tea party to cheer ourselves up.
I say, "Chérie"—that's French for "darling"—"you are
going to be the greatest oyster ever."

Bree says, "Nobody will be a better tree than you."

At the next dance class, we practice our parts. And guess what! I'm not just a plain old tree. Madame Lucille tells me to pretend I am a weeping willow.

"Willows are very graceful," Madame says. "Their branches swoop and sway and swirl in the wind."

I swoop and sway everywhere I go.

I make my face look very sad because
I am a weeping willow.

A week later, there is startling news.
Startling is fancy for surprising, only in a bad
way. Savanah, who is one of the mermaids, has sprained her
ankle. She cannot dance.

But Madame Lucille tells us, "Savanah can still be in the ballet. She will be one of the oysters, and . . .

…Bree will take Savanah's place as one of the mermaids."

Say what?!

Bree throws her arms around me. She is beaming. (That's smiling from ear to ear.)
"I'm so happy for you," I say. Only I don't really mean it.

I liked it much better when neither of us got to be a mermaid.

At home I stuff my beautiful costume in the back of my closet. My mermaid days are over!

When my mom comes to say good night, I tell her about Bree. "I'm a terrible girl. I lied. I said I was happy for her. And I'm not!"

"That's not lying, exactly. You want to be happy for Bree, don't you?" my mom asks me.

"Of course. She is my best friend!"

"It's just hard now because Bree got something you wanted very much. You're jealous. But your heart is so generous and warm, it will melt the bad feelings away."

I am 100 percent positive that my mom is the wisest mother in the world.

The next morning I give Bree my fanciest shell tiara.
"It's yours for keeps," I tell her.

"I wish we were both mermaids," she says.

Soon it is time to get ready. My costume is magnificent.

My branches are made of tinsel. And I wear a little nest in my hair. I am going to be the fanciest willow tree ever.

The ballet is a smashing success. (That's fancy for a big hit.) When it's my turn to dance, something happens.

I feel carried away by the music. I swoop and sway almost as if I were a real weeping willow.

At the end we all get a standing ovation. That means everyone jumps up and claps like crazy.

My parents give me a beautiful bouquet of flowers.

"Merci," I say. "Mom, you were right. It was thrilling to perform in a ballet."

We all go to the King's Crown to celebrate.
Bree and I toast each other. That means we
clink our glasses together and then we shout,

"Bravo for us!"